THE HEART OF A
CHAMPION

Five Easy Principles for Success and Happiness

Steve Karagioules

authorHOUSE®

AuthorHouse™
1663 Liberty Drive
Bloomington, IN 47403
www.authorhouse.com
Phone: 1 (800) 839-8640

Published by AuthorHouse 10/19/2018

ISBN: 978-1-5462-6531-3 (sc)
ISBN: 978-1-5462-6530-6 (e)

INTRODUCTION

I am not a millionaire, and I may never become one. While it can happen as a result of my work and dedication to my dreams, it will never be my definition of success. You may not have the same definition, and that is fine. How each of us defines our success should be personal and hopefully is based on ideas that define us and our ideas of happiness. I say *hopefully* because too many people work their lives for things that they realize too late actually don't make them happy.

If you're confused with my alternating use of the words *success* and *happiness*, it is because my definition of success is happiness. How can we declare to be successful if the success we've achieved actually brings us down? It can be argued that it's better to cry in a Lamborghini than it is on a bike or in a mansion versus a small apartment. And while those comparisons make sense, what about crying in a Lambo versus laughing on a bike? Or what about being lonely in a mansion versus being surrounded by loved ones in an apartment? You can have all the money in the world, the career achievements, and wonderful material things to go along with it, but what if it came at the cost of being truly happy?

These don't have to be choices though. There is no rule that says, if you are rich, you are automatically unhappy. In fact, I've met many people who have a lot of money and have also built lives for themselves that they are truly happy with. This comes from making the right choices in their lives and careers. They make the pursuit of their dreams more than just about how much money they make or what things they can collect. They made their happiness their goal, and as a result, they became rich, not the other way around.

Since the beginning of time, people like Alexander the Great, Cleopatra, Gandhi, and Martin Luther King Jr. have marked history with their exceptional dedication to their dreams. People chasing their dreams have resulted in humanity's improved standard of living, technological advances, medical treatments, and cures. History's great explorers and the cure for polio are just two examples. When people go after their dreams, great things happen.

The people who go after their dreams represent a small portion of life, both in history and today. Most people just go along with the way things are. Most people take what they can get. They accept the scraps swept off the table of life. They'll accept it as "just the way things are." At work, they accept their job and status quo and don't aspire for more. They may dream of more but aren't ready to invest the effort required to achieve it. They leave their lives to chance, floating through life like a rudderless ship with no direction and no destination.

This feeling of lack of control over our success and lives is a major cause of stress and other emotional or mental health problems. At work, it can lead to burnout, and outside of work, it can lead to depression. Within workplaces, it is often the cause of politics and backstabbing, as those who have accepted the status quo battle those who seek to improve it. Even the people who have ascended the corporate ladder don't necessarily ascribe to the mentality of champions. Like so many in life, they work to do enough to build their stock, but not enough to make things too difficult or challenging and ultimately rewarding.

Consider those who you've known or heard of who were unhappy with their level of physical fitness. I've known many, and very few dedicated a lasting and disciplined effort toward improving. They would prefer to live with their poor health or weight and make excuses than work through the difficulties and live happily with better physical fitness. They could look at themselves daily and think about how things would be if they could create a self-image that they're happy with and then go ahead and make all the excuses as to why they can't.

Of course, most of those excuses are things that are outside of their control and could be overcome if they simply chose to. Except they choose not to. Why? Why do only a small percentage of people go after their dreams? Why do only the exceptional few take the risks and put forth the efforts in order to get the successes they seek? Why, having been born with the ability to reach the stars, do most people not even stretch to try?

Michael Jordan was cut from his high school basketball team. He went home and cried. Then he told himself that it would be the last time he was ever cut from a team. And it was. His dominance in the NBA, now ranked amongst the best players in the world, is practically unparalleled in sports history.

Arnold Schwarzenegger came from rural Austria to become five-time Mr. Universe and seven-time Mr. Olympia. Despite a thick Austrian accent, he became one of the top-paying actors in Hollywood in the 1990s. He wasn't done there either. He then became governor of California, the sixth-largest economy in the world. Any one of those things would be enough for a lifetime. Arnie did them all. He dreamed to achieve all of them, even though people at every step doubted and discouraged him. More importantly, despite outside negativity, none existed in him. He battled against the obstacles and difficulties and became a life champion!

Those are only two examples of people who have gone after their dreams and got them and then some! These two people followed their hearts toward their passions and achieved massive success as a result. They remained focused on what was important for them despite going through exactly what everyone else in their situation would endure. The difference is the following:

- They pushed through; they didn't allow distractions to get in the way.
- They didn't put their efforts into making up excuses; they put them into succeeding.
- They didn't seek the easy path, the route of mediocrity and conformity; they took risks and chose the avenue toward their full potential.
- They didn't stay down when they got knocked down; they got back up and pushed on.
- They knew that the path toward mediocrity, while easier, led to a life with less profound happiness.

- They did what most people won't and don't do, but what all people are capable of.

The greats understand that you can't put out common efforts and expect uncommon results. By doing what most others won't, they achieve what most others don't.

There are many successful people in life, but what separates average success with greatness? Average success actually is often the biggest obstacle to great success, just as some happiness comes at the cost of great happiness. This is because average success is good. It can bring some riches and accolades and can be attained with a limited amount of effort.

Average success can also be a poisoned pill, which can lead to complacency. For too many, it leads to a life where we take it easy and fail to see our weaknesses because we take our success for granted. We fail to recognize what got us here in the first place. We start believing mystical things like destiny and talent and forget hard facts like hard work and continuous improvement. We rest on our laurels and accept being good at the demise of great.

In that, we find the distinguishing differences between the good and the greats:

- those who work tirelessly to live uplifted lives and those who accept the lives they can get with limited commitment
- those who understand that their competition can have a greater hunger for success if they allow them to
- those who understand that what they did to get them this far will not be enough to keep them

there and to keep the momentum going in the right
direction

The champions understand the following:

- The road to success doesn't get easier with time.
- Success is their only option.
- Achievement of their dreams and the path toward
  it will lead to a happier, successful life.

They also comprehend the truths of what I call the
"heart of a champion."

What makes them so special? Is it genetics? Intelligence?
Luck? Lineage? Upbringing? Wealth? Social status? One could
argue that Arnold Schwarzenegger had superior genetics,
which permitted him to win all of those bodybuilding
championships. However, you'd be very shortsighted if you
ignored the thousands of hours he invested in the gym.
You would be way off track if you overlooked his desire
to improve constantly and his commitment to becoming
champion. You may be born with similar morphology as
Arnold, but unless you put in the work required and had the
mind-set needed to be the best you that you could possibly
be, you're not coming anywhere close to a bodybuilding
championship, let alone as many as Schwarzenegger won.

Genetics do have a part in the greatness of athletes, but
their genetics also played a role in influencing their dream.
Yet their genetics did not play as much of a part as their
dedication to achieving their dreams did. Their dedication
drove their work ethic and pushed them past their peers. In
fact, all studies that looked at what influenced success the
most have shown that it has very little to do with any of the

previously mentioned factors. Genetics, intelligence, family, upbringing, wealth, social status, and even luck were not large determinants of success.

Instead, when looking at those who went after more and worked to achieve their full potentials in life, they all share certain undeniable facts, truths that make up what I call the "heart of a champion." We will look at each of them:

1. having a solid why
2. believing they can do it
3. working hard
4. never settling
5. having an obsession for success

We will see that everyone driven to become the best he or she can be adheres to these basics. And that is what sets these people apart from the rest.

Dream of Greatness

When my first daughter, Dahlia, was born, I remember being overcome with joy and hope. It was a feeling that I had never experienced. There was so much happiness in my heart that my eyes welled up and my voice trembled. My wife cried as she held our daughter for the first time, and we both were happier than ever before in our lives.

Our second daughter, Samara, was born twenty months later. I remember before her birth that I explained to my wife how I was afraid that there wasn't any space left in my heart for her because I loved Dahlia so much. She assured me that everything would work out. Sure enough, when I saw

Samara's big brown eyes for the first time, they completely enthralled me. I was once again filled with the greatest feeling of happiness and hope.

I believe any parent can identify with my story. Friends I grew up with, those who never displayed any form of love or tenderness to anything, became huge teddy bears with the birth of their children. Most parents will agree that there truly is nothing in life that inspires and brings joy like the birth of a child.

When a child is born, parents look upon that child with nothing but dreams of success, health, and happiness. We name our children with the thought of their peers holding their names in high regard. We dream of greatness for our children. I don't think that any father (or mother) looks down at his child and imagines an average life, an existence where the child can just get by and are somewhat happy, a life where the child doesn't reach his or her full potential but rather just does enough to get the bills paid.

No. Every father (or mother) dreams that his child will spread his or her wings and soar to heights that surpasses the parent's own. Parents dream of nothing but the best for their children and the ideal that they will overcome all challenges and leave their mark on the world.

After the birth of my girls, I wondered why parents dream of greatness and profound happiness for their children but limit themselves to mediocrity and fleeting happiness. Why do we expect our children to soar but expect the achievement of the status quo for ourselves? What kind of example is that? Why do so many people limit themselves to their current situations and realities but dream that their children will go further and reach higher? Why do we settle on security but pass up on greatness? Why accept the status quo at the expense of the new ideas and efforts? Why does safe beat out passion? Why does stability beat out reward? Why does being good beat out being great?

This book, *The Heart of a Champion*, aims to convince you to go for the greatness within you and to teach you how to reach your full potential, your greatness. I hope that these written pages will convince you to discover your true motivations and to go after them—to do so not only because of the potential to earn more and have more, but, more importantly, to discover a life that is enjoyed with a deep, lasting happiness, an ultimate success where you do what you love and love what you do.

Everyone's full potential is to be great, but most people don't reach it. Everyone could live a life of true success and happiness, but most don't put out the effort needed to have it. I believe that is the case because most people don't believe it's possible, think they have greatness within them, and know how to achieve it.

Dahlia, now eleven years old, came to me recently and declared that she wants to be a scientist when she grows up. She followed that statement with an even bolder one, saying that she would cure cancer. The hope I felt when she was born has never faded. I still believe that she and her sister can go farther than I ever have, and her statement provided me with a feeling of pride and hope.

As she sat before me at the kitchen table very matter-of-factly, I looked back at her and gave her the advice that I'll share with you. "I believe that you can, but more importantly, you must never stop believing that you can. If you can do that, you will."

CHAPTER 1

What is Success?

What is success? What makes a champion? How do people become great? There is no simple definition or example for success. Success, they say, is a journey, not a destination. But what does that mean? If you can't arrive at success, then how do you get there? It is extremely important to understand what success means in order to comprehend what we need to do to become successful. Let's look at some theory.

Abraham Maslow was an American psychologist most famously known for his 1943 psychological health theory, Maslow's hierarchy of needs. The theory defined human motivation as a pyramid that we move up or down, depending on whether the previous level's psychological needs have been met. The five levels of human motivational needs are, from bottom to top, physiological, safety, love/belonging, esteem, and self-actualization. Maslow proposed that one need, the more basic of needs, dominated the human organism.

Physiological Needs

If we don't meet our physiological needs, we die. These are our survival needs. These needs are pressing and spell our demise quickly if not met. Without them, we can't survive for long. We require things like food, water, oxygen, and shelter. These needs are thought to be the most important.

Safety Needs

Once the necessities of life are cared for, we can move on from our physiological needs to letting our safety needs dominate our thoughts and actions. People seek to live without war, disaster, crime, abuse, and poverty. Children have a higher level of safety needs. Think of the child who needs to be comforted because he or she is afraid of the dark. Typically children get over their fear as they age, along with many other safety needs. There are four different safety needs: personal security, financial security, health and well-being, and a safety net against accidents and illness and their adverse impacts.

Love and Belonging

Once people are surviving and feel safe, they need to feel a sense of belonging. Humans are social beings, as displayed by our need to communicate with other humans. It is also something felt stronger in children, as this need decreases as independence increases. Basically put, we want to be liked, and we want to feel like we fit in. Different people want to fit in with different sizes of groups, but still, all humans want to love and be loved. When these needs are not met, people can develop loneliness, anxiety, and depression.

Esteem

Now that you feel like you belong, you need to feel like others value you. Humans want to feel like their contributions are valued and they are respected. To satisfy this need, people will seek to gain recognition for their contributions. It is why people will go into certain high-profile professions.

Maslow divided our esteem needs into two: the external and the internal. I already mentioned the external. Internal self-esteem needs are higher-version esteem needs that include knowledge, strength, competence, mastery, independence, freedom, and self-confidence.

Self-Actualization

To describe this need, Maslow said, "What a man can be, he must be." This need is simply for the person to reach his or her full potential. People's full potentials are possible when they pursue things that draw them to dedicate their skills and knowledge at the highest level possible.

In his best-selling book, *Flow,* Mihaly Czikszentmihaly shows how people get into deep concentration on the task at hand when in flow, which occurs when the person is able to dedicate his or her efforts on something he or she truly loves.

Maslow theorized that people often became specific in their needs of self-actualization. They would look to become really good at one thing, such as parenting, a hobby, volunteering, or cycling. While they may also perform in other areas of their lives, the specific activity provides the feel of self-actualization.

The Hierarchy of Needs

Let's be clear: Maslow's theory isn't perfect and isn't without its detractors. Nonetheless, it still structures our needs in a way that makes sense. Ensuring that you have food in order to survive will be a bigger priority than mastering your passion for pottery. You'll also focus on your safety before concerning yourself with how many likes you received on your most recent Facebook post.

This isn't to say that lines don't get crossed sometimes. For example, a person may focus more on becoming independent than being loved, particularly in an environment where the individual feels like there is no love to receive. In general though, the hierarchy of needs provides a clear understanding of the types of needs we seek to satisfy as we fulfil other more basic ones.

In most industrialized countries, most people are not struggling to survive. Most of these societies are also relatively safe. This leaves people living there working to satisfy the higher-tier needs: love and belonging, esteem, and self-actualization. Here, we can begin to understand why so many people struggle to be happy and become successful.

If our most basic needs are satisfied, we should evolve our thinking in order to fulfil our other needs. However, we live in a society with less and less human connection due to technology as well as our busy lifestyles. Less human connection (because we're working so much or remaining immersed in our phones and apps) means that we have less of an opportunity to connect with those around us.

Have you ever seen a family having dinner at a restaurant, but no one is talking because every member of the family or both parents are busy with something on their phones? Have you ever seen a couple on a date with the same activity going on? If you haven't, it may be because you're too involved in whatever you have on your phone. It happens all the time!

As people lack love and belonging, their needs go unsatisfied unless they find another way to fulfil it. Advertising and suggestive selling then bombards them, and what does all that marketing around us tell us to do? Satisfy yourself by buying stuff! Become an endless consumer because all of that new stuff will make you happy!

Don't believe me? Pay attention to advertising and the message it conveys to you about who you become by using the product or service. The best examples are those cheap infomercials that play late at night. The product they are selling could be a simple cloth, but they make life before this cloth look like hell! Life with their marvelous product is better and easier.

Of course they wouldn't sell too many if they showed the opposite or demonstrated no obvious advantage for someone to change products for theirs. So naturally they'll show people being happy that their problems are solved. But what does that suggestion do to you? Particularly today, where Walker-Smith reported that people may be seeing as many as five thousand ads per day, what impact does the messaging play on your psyche subconsciously?

Do you have an iPhone 8? Don't you know that the Xs is out now with a bigger screen? What an amazing feature! You'll feel better by having the latest and greatest that you can show off to your friends, colleagues, and family.

And the message continuously bombards us—with more subtlety, of course—but the significance is clear. Buy more; be happy. So in that world, to get the things, you need money. So money equals more things, and more things equal success. Many people believe this subconsciously. Openly, they may say they don't value money but indebt themselves heavily to have a full lifestyle. Then there are those who openly seek to purchase the best things, regardless of the cost, and will sacrifice everything for their wealth.

It's not to say that having nice things and money are bad. They're not. Working hard and reaping the rewards are any person's rights. I support anyone trying to make an honest living. My statements have more to do with the cost that having the things and getting more money incurs on so many people. Debt is all around us because, as a society, it has become okay to owe money for things that we don't need.

Needs are things like food, water, shelter, and safety, not Nikes, iPhones, two-car garages, and the latest sport coupe. These material things end up costing so much that most people become stuck chasing the dollar instead of enjoying their lives. Most Americans live paycheck to paycheck. An interruption of earning can have a devastating effect on most families in the United States and Canada. The

Canadian personal debt statistics tell us where we've gone in Western society.

In 1990, Canadians owed eighty-five cents for every dollar of disposable income.[1] In 2017, it has climbed to $1.63 per dollar of disposable income. That means that, after the average Canadian has paid his or her taxes and deductions have been taken from his or her paycheck, what's left could only cover a little over half of what he or she owes. Hopefully, these people are still paying for their food, water, and shelter.

We can't really only be about money, business, and work, can we? I'm all for working hard and earning a great living, but how successful can someone feel if he or she is lonely? What if a person feels like he or she could do more, as if something were missing in his or her life? Western society has more wealth today than ever before. People own more than they ever have in history. Yet most individuals are unhappy with their lives. They're simply going through the motions.

Researchers found that, while Americans earn more than they did thirty years ago, they are less happy due to longer working hours and the deterioration of the quality of relationships between neighbors and friends. Clearly, money and material belongings alone aren't enough to provide profound happiness.

So as people try to satisfy their need for love and belonging with more material possessions, they can actually trick their brains into believing that more stuff actually

---

[1] Danielle Webb and Tavia Grant, "Canada's Borrowing Binge," http://www.theglobeandmail.com/globe-investor/personal-finance/household-finances/canadian-households-now-owe-a-record-18-trillion-and-more-debt-statistics/article24322565.

makes them happy. This means that they could also move up the hierarchy and try to satisfy their esteem needs.

Satisfying the need for recognition has changed over the years. In Abraham Maslow's time, people mastered their craft, studied for years, or worked extremely hard to be the best at something. It now can take very little to get noticed through social media for all the wrong reasons. Produce one extreme video, and you can get millions of views and thousands of shares, likes, and comments. All that attention can make it feel like people really respect you and like you. For instance, take that girl who told people, "Catch me outside. How 'bout dat?" She became famous for all the wrong reasons at thirteen years old! Can you imagine how this will warp this girl's perception of reality (even further than it already was)?

Another way other people try to get famous through social media is by trolling a celebrity in hopes that it will get them noticed. They work hard to appear so clever in hopes of building a little following with the goal of making a career out of it. Whatever the method, social media has made the esteem need easy to superficially satisfy, again leaving many people feeling as if they've fulfilled their needs.

Unfortunately, not many people make it to self-actualization for a number of reasons:

1. If you're so busy paying off the debts you've accumulated from buying the things that you didn't need in the first place, how can you afford to take the risk and do what truly makes you whole?

2. When you are so busy working and some of your needs have been artificially been satisfied, will you really know what your purpose is?

Chances are, if you've bought into the consumerism society wholeheartedly, you've also bought into their sales pitch, which wants you to lose yourself and just focus on the things that will make you happier.

What happens to people whose fundamental needs are artificially satisfied? Consider our survival needs. What would happen if, instead of nutritious food, you ate food void of any nutrition? Well at first your body would be tricked, thinking that the food it was receiving was good. You wouldn't feel hungry, so your alarm bells would stop sounding. With time though, your body would suffer from malnutrition, and eventually if not rectified, you'd die.

What about the falsely satisfied love and belonging or esteem needs? What happens to the person who believes that his or her followers online are friends and cares for them until he or she gets trolled? Or what about the person who devotes his or her time and energy to become a YouTube star but can't make a splash or, worse, gets trounced in the comments?

What happens is that you end up with a lot of people who are lost about how to find satisfaction with their lives. Individuals are at the end of their rope as they work harder and harder to keep up but find no lasting happiness in the things they own. Again, consider the Italian study[2] that showed

---

[2] Deepa Babington, "Americans Less Happy Than 30 Years Ago," http://www.reuters.com/article/us-happiness-usa-idUSL155 0309820070615.

Americans were less happy because they worked more and had fewer interactions with neighbors and friends, despite earning more money.

So what does all of this have to do with becoming successful? Success has a lot more to do with properly satisfying our psychological needs than our financial ones. This is proven when considering the difference in happiness between a person earning $5,000 per year and the individual earning $50,000. Which person do you think is happier? Do you think that there is a big difference? What about someone earning $50,000 versus someone earning $5 million? Studies have shown that, while the person making $50,000 is much happier in life than the individual making only $5,000, there isn't much difference between the $50,000 and the $5 million. Why is that?

Money, like other material things, are known as hygiene factors. In motivation, they are considered as external factors. Like washing your hair with shampoo or brushing your teeth doesn't keep you alive, they work to make you healthier. Except you wouldn't have any added benefit if you washed your hair three times a day. In fact, it would probably have an adverse effect on your health.

Money works the same way. Up to a certain point, it will provide more for us and make us happier, partly because it satisfies our two first needs, survival and safety. After that, money cannot make you more loved or, in itself, make people respect or hold you in high esteem. Money can make life more comfortable, but it can also make life a lot busier and stressful. As the returns on happiness from more money diminish, stress levels, less free time, and weaker relationships increase.

Money is the determinant of success. Money also must be balanced with the higher-level needs, which are to find love and belonging within a group, to gain the respect of others, and to reach your potential in the thing that makes you best. This means having time and energy to invest with family and friends and doing something that makes you proud and gaining the respect of others for it. And it means doing the thing in life that you do best.

When you set goals that you aspire to complete, remember to make them balanced throughout your life. Stephen Covey has a good technique in the *7 Habits of Highly Effective People*, whereas you first determine your roles in life. The roles define you as a person, but each may have different needs and approaches. Once your roles are defined, you establish a vision for success in each.

For example, two of my roles are as father and business leader. My vision of success as a father involves my relationships with my children and their mother; my vision as a business leader still involves relationships with my employees. It also involves the kind of money and business success I aspire to. Once the visions are established, you can set long- and short-term goals in order to work toward the visions of success.

Not having goals allows you to fall into the endless cycle of work and consumerism. Setting SMART[3] goals based on your visions of success in your various roles allows you to have targets to aim for success in the numerous aspects of your life. Doing so helps more people find balance than otherwise

---

[3] SMART stands for Specific, Measureable, Achievable, Relevant, and Time-Based.

floating through life aimlessly, which leads too many people to depression and anxiety.

As humans, expensive things don't impress our happiness for long. Our happiness lies in the balance of satisfying our higher needs of love and belonging, esteem, and self-actualization. We need to be building deeper human relations, feel like we're helping others by contributing, and do what makes us great.

It is easy to write and say. However, working for a life where we have the freedom to do the things that matter most, like invest time with our children without being interrupted by our phones buzzing or ringing, doesn't happen by accident. People who live more fulfilled lives don't stumble into it by accident. Getting there takes hard work.

Whether the hard work is coming from giving up on some of the material comforts that people have gotten used to in order to live simpler lives or working harder on their plan to be able to build their dreams, it is hard work. Happiness is a choice, but success is hard work.

CHAPTER 2

The Path of Least Resistance

What happens when someone tells you that he or she is going to get something done but doesn't? This person comes up with excuses! It isn't always malicious or even purposeful. Often they are the reasons and excuses that the person has sold himself or herself to make it all acceptable. The individual creates excuses so he or she can continue living with himself or herself and not allow his or her failure to weigh on him or her. What happens after the person has bought his or her own excuses? He or she tries to sell them to you and others around him or her!

What would happen if people worked harder at reaching their full potential than they do at the excuses for why they don't? You would have a whole lot more people working harder! Not only that, so many people would be doing what they love. Or at the very least, so many more people would be happier with their lives and themselves. Instead of taking the easier path, which is not the route to happiness, success (or greatness), they would be working at achieving what they want from their lives.

But that is hard. It is easier to make excuses why you don't exercise than it is to actually work out. It is easier to make excuses why you can't go back to school than it is to hunker down and go to night classes like I did. It is easier to hate your job and complain about it than it is to quit your position and go after your full potential. It's easier than simply going for something better.

It's easier to point the finger at others as why you aren't where you ought to be than it is to suck it up, take responsibility for your own actions and decisions, come up with a plan, and go after it with all you have. It's easier to quit when the going gets tough, you fall, or you've suffered a setback.

The easy way is always an attractive option. Of course, you could watch television in the evening, and you'd have a ton of reasons (pronounced *excuses*) why that is ok. However, you could use that time more productively, like writing the book you've been dreaming of compiling, planning the business you always wanted to start, taking the language class you wanted to learn, or hitting the gym (or even going out for a walk or run).

The easy way is always calling, particularly louder when things get tough. Except nothing great was ever achieved on the easy path. If your intention is to go after your full potential, you're going to have to work hard at avoiding the easy way, the path of least resistance.

You may have heard of an old Native American legend that describes the battle we all face internally about whether to be positive and face our obstacles and challenges or to be negative and allow ourselves to be mired in negativity, worry, and doubt. In the legend, an old man is talking to his grandson about life and tells him that inside every person there is a battle that rages between two wolves. The first wolf is the Good Wolf; he represents positivity, confidence, faith, honesty, happiness, compassion, and all that is good. The second is the Bad Wolf; he represents negativity, doubt, anger, envy, deceit, fear, and all that is bad.

The old man explains to the young boy that the two wolves battle every day, and as he finishes telling the story, the boy asks, "Which one wins?"

To which the old man replies, "Whichever one you feed."

This is the best representation of what happens to us every day. We are constantly battling between doing things the right way or the easy way. The wolf we feed gets bigger and stronger, meaning, if we always give in to the one that avoids difficulties and remains negative, it progressively becomes harder to change that.

Say you don't just want to settle in life, that you want to pursue your greatness in anything. You will not reach your goals by taking the easy path. You will need to work hard and to face the challenges associated with becoming great. We are not naturally developed to face challenges and work through adversity. The Bad Wolf is naturally bigger and meaner. This is human nature, that is, the desire to take the path of least resistance. We naturally want to avoid things that we don't like, things that hurt us (physically, mentally, or emotionally) and things we fear. This avoidance is an innate survival mechanism.

Due to this natural tendency, the Bad Wolf has years of feeding, and depending on the person, it may have been a really long time since the Good Wolf has won a battle. To be able to begin on the path to greatness, instead of the path of least resistance, it will be very hard at first. The Good Wolf needs to build its strength and be fed, and the Bad Wolf must be starved. While trying to feed the Good Wolf, the Bad Wolf will try to convince you otherwise. His voice will be in your head as doubts and fears that will scream louder as things get harder. And it will get harder.

But there is hope. The Good Wolf can also be fed and developed. With time, it too can get stronger and louder. You just need to keep feeding it. Start with overcoming small challenges and obstacles. At first, it may not even matter if you overcome those challenges. Simply accept that you're pushing yourself, that you're feeding your Good Wolf. As the Good Wolf grows and gets stronger and bolder, your level of confidence will rise. As it does, pushing yourself will get easier. The challenges may not, but accepting to take on the challenge versus taking the path of least resistance in order to achieve more will.

I noticed this in my own life when I began doing Spartan Races, mountainside obstacle courses that range from five to fifty kilometers long. I originally signed up because I was bored at the gym. I didn't completely avoid the difficult path since I've always worked hard and exercised three to four times per week. However, deep down, there was a desire for more. I could feel that I lacked the motivation to train hard. I was at a pretty good fitness level, but as I mentioned earlier, good is the enemy of great. I wanted a target that would oblige me to push harder and get into great shape.

My first race was the Spartan Super, a thirteen-plus kilometer race at Mont Tremblant in Quebec. I figured that, if I did a race that wasn't a given to complete—which was my feeling for the Sprint, which is only five kilometers long—I would have to get out of my comfort zone when working out. There was no doubt about the grind required in training in order to succeed in the races.

In preparation for the races and of course in completing the races over the years, it has allowed me to feed the Good Wolf. Whenever the Bad Wolf would tell me that I had done enough or that my muscles were too tired to keep going, I resisted the temptation to give up. In doing so, my Good Wolf grew. Now there is less fear of failure in my heart. I have learned the benefits of stretching outside of my comfort zone to achieve more. My Bad Wolf is still there. The battle continues. However with conditioning and practice, my Good Wolf has been fed. When the Bad Wolf tells me to take the easy path, my Good Wolf responds with a thundering "no!"

No matter what you do, the easy way will always be calling. Our nature is to avoid things we dislike, and humans dislike fear the most. The fear of failure says, "What if I fail? What will people think of me?" And the fear of success says, "What if I succeed and I can't handle it?"

If you don't take on your challenges and feed the right habits (the Good Wolf), you will naturally want to take the path of least resistance, the easy route (to do what the Bad Wolf wants). You will avoid what you dislike: fear, difficulty, hard work, setbacks, and ultimately becoming great, that is, becoming a champion. Instead you will make excuses that you will sell to yourself and try to sell to others.

CHAPTER 3

What is a Champion?

There are a lot of books and videos on the topic of success. But what is success? It can be defined in so many ways. Is it financial? Many would say that the money you bring in or the amount in your bank account determine your greatness. Or is success about fame and glory? Others would argue that, when you become the best in your field, you will be recognized and become known for your work. Is it about prizes and awards? Some might say, "Unless you've been recognized as the best, how could you be a champion?"

I can understand all of those points but don't agree with any of them entirely. For me, success is being great at whatever you choose to be great at, whatever is truly important to you. Being great is to be strong enough to not have to follow the definitions provided to you by society, your friends, your family, or your peers. Being great is setting a target for yourself in something that captures your heart and your head and achieving it. Then you set a new target and achieve it. And so on.

In some fields of life, it is easy to define a champion. A professional boxer is a champion when he or she holds the belt. An Olympic swimmer wins the gold. But not everyone aspires for sports greatness. There are no gold medals for being a super parent. That doesn't mean you can't be a champion mom or a great husband. In business, you could become the richest person in the world. But are you not a champion business leader if you aren't? Of course not. You can do what was unthinkable: become the best in your industry, city, or franchise group.

I personally admire all of the athletes that make it to the pinnacle of their careers. In fact, all of those who make it to the Olympics are the best from their countries and the best in the world. Being a champion isn't about hardware or glory. Sugar Ray Leonard said, "A champion doesn't become champion in the ring; he's only recognized there."

Being great, that is, being a champion, is all about the work ethic and the journey. Being a champion is being the best you can be, reaching your potential. Not everyone can win the gold, but champions go for it despite the odds. In the face of adversity, challenges, obstacles, and odds, champions keep going. They keep fighting.

In Norse mythology, there is the legend of the Ragnarok apocalypse. In the legend, the gods were faced with their inevitable demise. The end of life had been foretold to the gods, and they knew that, regardless of their actions, their end was quickly approaching. The gods, including Odin, Thor, and Tyr, could have retired to Asgard to relax and await their fate.

Except they were gods. They would not allow the world to be engulfed in flames and war. Despite their fate, they fought. In the face of their ultimate loss and the impossible odds, the gods did battle in order to save the world. One of the points of the legend was to instill the ideas into the Vikings (those who created the wonderful Norse mythology) that, regardless of the odds they could face, they must never surrender and never stop fighting.

This is the essence of the heart of a champion:

- Believing in yourself and pushing to be the best you can
- Not surrendering to circumstance, status quo, or odds
- Not accepting your current self
- Being like Jim Rohn describes, "Like a tree"

The principle of growing like a tree means to grow as much as you can. Mr. Rohn explains that the tree grows as much as possible and not when it decides to stop. Only humans decide to stop growing by failing to learn, read, and challenge themselves.

Another parallel between the tree and people is that we go through seasons. Where I'm from in Canada, trees are dormant in the cold and darkness of the winter. As the light lasts longer and days and nights get warmer, the tree awakes and begins to blossom. At the peak of the summer, it flourishes and grows quickly, and it finally slowly goes back to sleep as the cold and darkness return in the fall. People also go through cycles that resemble the seasons in our lives. We can go through periods of hard times where nothing seems to work. Persistence and not losing faith allows us to climb out of the darkness and cold and revive our results and productivity.

The champion, like the gods of Norse mythology or the mighty tree, is propelled by confidence in oneself and continues on his or her path to grow and reach his or her full potential. The sports star can be a champion, and so can the single mom. The Fortune 500 business leader can be a champion, and so can the small business owner. The marathon runner can be a champion, and so can the middle-aged man on his own training program.

So what do the most successful people and teams have in common? Throughout history's greatest upsets, most triumphant victories, biggest champions, and driven leaders all shared certain undeniable facts that led them to their success, facts that I call the "heartbeats of a champion."

CHAPTER 4

First Heartbeat—Champions Have Fuel for Their Fire

The path to becoming a champion is a difficult and lonely journey. It is lonely in many ways because it is difficult. Many people haven't found what it takes to get started. Even more haven't found what it takes to continue when the going gets tough. Most people don't reach their goals (that is, don't become champions) because they haven't found the right fuel to light their way on the path to greatness when it becomes dark.

When many people start thinking of stretching in their lives, the initial idea lights a small fire within them. This fire provides them with the motivation to dream. They begin imagining what life would be like if they succeed. Regardless of how big or small the dream is, there is a positive image of how the person will feel when he or she has succeeded. The individual finds a new bounce to his or her step, and in addition to dreaming of succeeding, this person begins telling people what he or she is up to.

We've all heard it and even said it, "I'm writing a book/going to lose weight/going to go back to school." Those around feel happy for them and, unless they're jealous, believe their proclamations of eventual success.

This is the typical start of a journey toward greatness. What separates the winners from the losers is what happens when they get smashed in the face with reality. In our dreams, the path to success appears short, brightly lit, and smooth as silk. The actual path is long, often very dark, and about as smooth as a pothole-filled street of Montreal in the spring. (Believe me, it's bad.) As Eric Thomas says, "If it were easy, everybody would do it."

There are always setbacks and difficulties, and most people aren't prepared for them. Many get hit with reality and quit. Reality is sometimes simply a realization of the fact that nothing will be given to them. In actuality they will need to work hard to make it. Want to write a book? It takes a sustained effort to get all of your thoughts on paper. Want to lose weight? It means you'll need to get up off your ass, work out, sweat, feel some pain, and change your eating habits. Want to go back to school? You'll have to attend, study, work, learn, and, if you're an adult, do all of it while juggling your other responsibilities. Even when people understand what they need to do to succeed, they fail to realize how much fuel they need in the tank to be able to get through it.

With no fuel, you are destined to fail before you even get started. Without enough fuel, you will not make it to your destination. With the correct fuel, it will keep you fired up throughout your journey, and you can far exceed your own expectations. The million-dollar questions then are: what is the fuel, and how do you get it?

The fuel is simply your reason for doing whatever it is that you're seeking to do. Why do want to write a book? Why do you want to lose weight? Why are you going back to school? Why do you want to achieve more? Why do you want to be a great parent? Why do you want to succeed in your own business? They seem like simple questions to answer except that, like everything on the path to greatness, nothing is easy.

Let me explain. If someone told you he or she wanted to write a book and you asked this person why, without much thought, he or she would probably answer, "I want to make lots of money or perhaps earn a passive income." Someone looking to lose weight might say, "I want to look better and/ or feel better." The person who says that he or she wants to go back to school may respond, "I want to develop the skills to work in another field or earn more money in my current job."

None of these answers are wrong since they are all personal, but none of them are deep enough. They don't provide the depth needed to fuel the whole journey. To get that, people need to dig deeper to find the real reason they want it.

Perhaps a man wanting to write the book is looking for a passive income so he can work less. Thus, he can invest more time with his children while still providing as much or more. His kids can enjoy time with their father while also getting the best of things in life, which the would-be author finds important as he had neither time with his parents nor the best of anything.

Maybe a woman who wants to lose weight wants to look better so she can feel better with what she sees in the mirror. Thus, she can have more confidence and happiness. Perhaps a man going back to school wants to so he can increase his earnings so he can move to a better neighborhood where he can live without fear of his own safety. Thus, he can raise his children in a more positive environment.

The reasons why people set out on great journeys simply don't lie in the reasons found on the surface. They are rooted in our deeper fears, beliefs, values, and dreams. To effectively expose and understand them, we need to dig. Most people don't really just want to be rich. They envision a future without stressing about bills or having to make difficult choices between things they want and need with their limited budget. If they had money, they would have less stress.

Often they envision providing a better life for their families and even friends. You'll very often hear stories of professional athletes and other financially successful people tell the story of how happy they were to be able to give more to their parents. There's the story of a teenage developer who cashed in big when his app began raking in loads of cash and paid off his parents' mortgage. Many people say they want money but dream of what they would make those funds do for them. They have a deeper desire that fuels them.

For me, my children fuel a lot of my motivations. This isn't uncommon for parents, particularly those like me who grew up having less than the other kids. My parents were from the old school and made do with hard work. They lived poor their whole lives and never completed high school, each of them obliged to go out and earn their keep. My father grew up in World War II Greece; my mother was raised in poor, rural Quebec.

My father and mother both worked very hard for their four kids. And my father would send money back home to take care of his mother and two sisters. There wasn't much time for family vacations; nor was there the money. It wasn't all gloom. While my parents weren't the touchy-feely types, I was lucky enough to never doubt my parents' love for me.

They supported me, and I could feel they were proud. For that, I believe I developed into the hardworking, goal-driven, and happy man that I am today. I appreciate whatever I have earned because I know what life is like with less. My two girls already enjoy more than I had, I think, both financially and emotionally. We live in a nice house in the city, the girls attend a good school, and we vacation regularly. We're also able to invest a lot of time with each other. We play games, go for bike rides and walks, have regular family outings, and work to keep communication open.

My motivation to earn more is driven by being able to give my girls more of what I have been giving. With more money, particularly earned through passive income, we can enjoy more of life together, not necessarily through material goods, although not without some either, but also with experiences and time.

The Five Whys

I learned this process a few years back in regards to problem solving in leadership and management. It is a simple process of getting to the root cause of a problem. Managers were encouraged to resist reacting to a performance problem without first investigating further. Doing so would avoid wasting time and money on implementing solutions that fall short because the root cause hadn't been resolved.

Instead it was recommended that managers learn the "why" to the problem and keep asking five times in an attempt to discover the real issue. Whether you'd actually have to ask five whys wasn't the point. It was to instill the habit of reflection before reaction.

The same process can be applied to our desires and dreams. To avoid trying to climb a ladder that is leaning on the wrong wall, go through the process of asking the five whys for the things you want to go for. Without asking, there is a higher chance of not seeing it out until success. People are more likely to give up on their goals without the right motivation. Questioning our desires allows us to zero in on our real why.

Knowing our real why allows us to

- remind ourselves when the going gets tough of why we started in the first place;
- simply grin and ignore the doubters and haters who don't see the possibilities that we do; and
- have a reason larger than our "why nots."

The harder the journey, the more the "why nots."

Here is an example of the questioning process: I want to run a marathon. Why? Because I want to show that I am still in great physical shape. Why? Because as I get older, my physical fitness becomes more important. Why? Because

27

I would like to remain active with my family and friends for as long as possible. Why? Because they mean a lot to me, they make me happy, and I would be very lucky to be around them for a long time. Why? Because I'd like to be around for a long time, as healthy as possible.

There is the root. The root desire in the preceding example to keep the fire burning until success is achieved is a very deep emotion of survival, love, and happiness. I want to live a long, healthy life, and my family and friends are a big part of it. Being around them in health makes me truly happy, and I will do what it takes to protect that. I will also go out and fight for it because it is so important to me, which is why the deeper dream of living actively with my loved ones until I'm "old and gray" has pushed me to go for more, like the Spartan Race Trifecta that I completed last year at the age of forty.

Many people want to train three to four times a week but keep being "too busy" to go. While they may have all the right reasons on the occasion, when it becomes more often than not, their doubts and fears distract them from the task at hand. This is why people join a gym, get a program through a personal trainer, and show up four days a week for one month. Then in month two, they miss a couple days. By the third month, they're missing one to two days per week, and by the fourth month, they stop going altogether. Perhaps you know this person. Possibly it is you. Maybe it isn't about going to the gym. For you, it is something else.

We all have different areas of life where we'll procrastinate simply because the why isn't big enough for us to change our behavior. One example, for me, was going to sleep at a more reasonable hour. Instead of going to bed with my wife at a reasonable hour, say 10:00 to 11:00 p.m., I stayed up to work and/or watch TV (often both) until 1:00 a.m. I wouldn't have the same jump getting out of bed, and although I was up and going within the hour, I'm sure my performance (brain power) was diminished.

I would start going to bed at a more reasonable hour, and then if I'd stay up one or two nights, the frequency would increase. It is as if, when you start giving in, you feed your Bad Wolf and give it power. It then becomes easier to back off from your commitments as the Bad Wolf—your doubts, fears, and the procrastination they cause—grows.

Your reason why is the key in overcoming your doubts. Take the example of my sleeping habits: why did I want to sleep at a more reasonable hour? I feel like I have more energy when I sleep earlier. I also feel happier, and I get more things done. Sleeping earlier puts me into the same cycle as the rest of my family, and with the increased energy and happiness, I enjoy my time with them even more.

Once I wrote down my reasons why I wanted to change some of the bad habits and add new good habits, I started getting more done. I would simply write down my top three to four reasons why I wanted to change on some of the things, and every morning I'd review them at breakfast. (I used to skip breakfast all the time, and it is another bad habit that I overcame.)

Every morning I would remind myself of the things I was working for and why I was doing it. I now sleep earlier on a normal basis but occasionally stay up because I do enjoy staying up and watching TV! When you have the right reasons, remind yourself every day why you're doing it until that thing becomes something you can't live without.

What are your root causes? What are your deep beliefs, values, and reasons to go after your dreams? To achieve greatness, you will need to do extraordinary things. To do those extraordinary things, you will need to overcome extraordinary obstacles. It is a simple equation. Any vehicle that travels a long journey needs the fuel to complete it. The greater the destination, the harder and longer the journey is and the more fuel that is needed. Determining the true motivations at your core will give you that fuel. It will propel you through hardship and setbacks. It will shield you from criticism and ridicule. It will speak louder than the negative internal voice. And it will reward you with giving you exactly what you truly desired.

Buster Douglas

Buster Douglas was a little-known heavyweight boxer who was offered up to "Iron" Mike Tyson as an easy payday. The fight was only meant to keep Mike Tyson busy while a serious contender could be found.

In the eighth round, Tyson did what he had done to every previous opponent he had faced. He pounded Douglas and sent him to the mat. Except, before the referee could count to ten, Buster Douglas was saved by the bell. On shaky legs, Douglas returned to his corner. The world waited for the next round and the inevitable—for Mike Tyson to do what he had done every time before, to knock out Buster Douglas.

The championship match was the biggest opportunity in Buster Douglas' career. He was a heavy underdog, except to his mother, who already thought he was the champ. She told everyone she could that her son would beat Mike Tyson and win the heavyweight title. Douglas was upset by his mom's proclamations and asked her to stop. However, with two days to go until the fight, Buster Douglas' mother died. In her final moments, he gave his word to his mother that he would win against Mike Tyson.

The world had given up on Buster Douglas. Everyone counted him out. No one expected him to make it out of the next round. No one except one person, Buster Douglas. As he sat in his corner, having just been saved by the bell, he remembered his why. Instead of returning to the ring like a pig going to its slaughter, Buster Douglas went back with the fight of a person whose reason why was greater than his reason why not.

Douglas would dominate the next two rounds, and in the tenth, for the first time in Mike Tyson's career, he felt the blow that would send him to the mat for the ten count, and Buster Douglas was crowned undisputed heavyweight champion of the world.

Without a solid why, Buster Douglas would have lost in the eighth. He would have lacked the fire needed to get back up and fight back to win. Instead the thought of not fulfilling his final promise to his dying mother was bigger than him. It was bigger than his fears and doubts and the doubts of the boxing world. Buster Douglas had the fuel that kept his fire burning in the darkest moment and pushed him to become the champion.

In the post-fight interview, Buster was asked how he was able to win the fight despite the fact that no one thought he could. His emotional response, "Because of my mother, God rest her heart."

Enjoy the Journey

Your fuel is your why—your purpose and your reason. Having the right why does more than simply give you the fuel to see your goals through. They also make the ride more enjoyable. The little successes have a greater impact and make the losses less. Progress, as little as it can be, is recognized as progress in the right direction.

Deeper desires are also less likely to be solid points that can be reached. They are long-living aspirations like happiness, quality of life, and financial ease. Therefore while goals can be set and reached on the path toward the deep desire, there will likely never be a final destination. For example, could you say, "That's enough happiness in my life. I have arrived"? Of course not. Happiness is a choice in accepting the life we live and supported by living the life we choose. It is achieved by the doing!

With the right why, the journey becomes the reward. That is why people keep going for more after they've already succeeded. They enjoy the path to greatness and who they become in the process, so there is no reason to stop. It is the reason why people who lose weight and adopt a healthy lifestyle continue after they've achieved their target. They end up enjoying the process. It is the reason why people who reach a certain level of financial success continue. They get their pleasure from the process. Those who've never gone after their dreams would accuse them of greed, and in some cases, they would be correct. But in most cases, the money they earn is no longer the object. It is the thrill of succeeding at more challenges. Will you stop when you attain your target weight, earnings, or lifestyle? Probably not. And it's because it won't be the reward that keeps you going. Instead it will be the chase, the hunt, and the journey.

These are also ways to know you've found the right purpose, fuel, or reason why. When you're doing the difficult things in life versus taking the easy path, your mind can be your worst enemy. It will question your abilities and reasoning and make you doubt yourself. Without the right fuel, you will believe those doubts because the process will not have a pleasant aspect to it. However, with the correct fuel, you will still find pleasure in the process, no matter how difficult it is or how lonely you feel. You'll find pleasure because you'll know you are working toward something that you want deep down. And that will propel you further.

It all boils down to this: to become great, that is, to become a champion in life, you must be willing to do what others won't and don't do. The path is not easy, so you need the right fuel in the tank to get through it. The fuel is your why. They are your reasons, and the right ones will provide you with the needed fuel to fulfill your journey until success.

CHAPTER 5

Second Heartbeat—Champions Believe in Themselves

The belief in yourself often comes as a by-product of the right fuel. Once you have a reason greater than yourself to achieve your full potential, you will feel that there is no other option but success. Buster Douglas made a promise to his dying mother, and when the world doubted him, he kept believing.

Stories of the greats being alone in their belief in themselves are quite common. One of the best stories is that of one of my idols, the great Les Brown, now a world-renowned motivational speaker and best-selling author. His beginnings were some of the worst we could imagine in North America. He was born in complete poverty, and by the grace of God, his adoptive mother, Mammy Mae, took him in.

Growing up, Les was labeled "retarded," and other students often picked on him. He was lucky enough to have a loving home and a few good teachers who didn't believe the labels and showed him that neither should he. Mr. Brown learned to work hard, and through an undying persistence, he became a radio DJ. Later in his career, when he began preaching to people about following their dreams and achieving their potential, he hit some hard times. He lost his home and was forced to sleep in his office. All of his peers and those who knew of his situation ridiculed him: how could Les Brown preach about becoming great when he was a step from being homeless?

Les Brown, however, never stopped believing. He knew that he just needed to keep ploughing away and eventually he would break through. For Mr. Les Brown, he believed that there was only one option possible. Today, he is one of the most successful motivational speakers and authors in the world. He was able to buy his mother her own house where the rain didn't come through the roof, and he owns a very successful business coaching company. Les Brown is a true success story considering from how far he's come, and it has so much to do with his unwavering belief in himself.

Steve Jobs said it best when he stated, "Everything around us in that you call life was made by people who were no smarter than you." I love this statement because, although so many people consider Jobs as a genius, he openly admitted that he is nothing special. All of the best in the varying fields have suffered failure and rebounded because they believed that they could do better.

I had the misfortune of losing my job three times in ten years. I quickly found other jobs the first two times with higher salaries so the layoffs were blessings. The third time, however, I searched for eight months and couldn't find anything. As my desperation grew, so did my belief that I would need to take control of my future versus leaving it in the hands of hiring managers.

So I started a pool fencing business in Montreal. I worked day and night and went into debt to get it off the ground, but the feeling of building a business that provided me with every dollar I needed to take care of my family was phenomenal. More than dollars, my business success provided me with the deep-seated belief that I could achieve anything that I set my heart and mind to. I realized that I was worth more than I knew prior to my unemployment.

Without a job and with a mortgage, car payments, two kids in private school, and a wife who had also lost her job, failure wasn't an option. My why was huge! I grew up with very little, and I was damned to have to return to that. I knew that life wouldn't end if we needed to liquidate; however, I wasn't giving up an inch without fighting with everything I had. Three years later, I continue to climb my hill to success. Every New Year provides new opportunities for more success. I know I have a lot more hill to climb and the only obstacle that can stop me is me.

I am nothing special, just an average guy working to achieve my best. My results are not average because I don't aim for average. I believe in my abilities to get more done than the average person. I don't know you. You can be reading this in California, Canada, Toronto, or Timbuktu. But there are some things that I know about you. You breathe air, you bleed red blood, you will die one day, and you can be great at whatever you set your heart on before that day. Greatness isn't just something that has been reserved for a select few in life; greatness isn't for those with superior intelligence, genetics, or great luck. No, luck is something that champions know is gained through hard work. A champion believes that he or she can win, that he or she can reach his or her goal. The greats believe that failure isn't a real possibility as long as they keep pushing and remain devoted.

You can read about great leaders like Winston Churchill who succeeded despite great odds and did so because they didn't have a plan B. They had no other plan because they believed that their plan A would work. It had to! In Churchill's famous speech before the British parliament, he stated,

> I have, myself, full confidence that if all do their duty, if nothing is neglected, and if the best arrangements are made, as they are being made, we shall prove ourselves once more able to defend our island home, to ride out the storm of war, and to outlive the menace of tyranny, if necessary for years, if necessary alone.

He believed that the resolve of the people of the United Kingdom would survive the assault of the Axis army, despite the war having not gone their way until then. His belief and, as a result, his leadership, was the turning point in the second World War and eventually led to our victory over the fascist armies of Mussolini and Hitler.

As I mentioned earlier, I may not know you, but I know you have greatness in you just as you have blood pumping in your veins. I know you have greatness because I have seen average people who, through great effort and belief in themselves, have achieved extraordinary success. I'm not speaking of extraordinary people. I'm talking about normal everyday people like you and I.

We are all born equal as humans. Our circumstances are different. Our appearances and beliefs may be different, but we are still the same. In many ways, our similarities lie in our differences. Riches have been squandered, and many more have risen from poverty. What we do in life depends completely on what we are going to do with it. Upon understanding that some people might have been born with better circumstances, that is only a factor of resources and not resourcefulness.

The person with the right fire and belief in his or her abilities to succeed will find ways to win where none existed before. I'm writing all this to say that, no matter where you are coming from or what your history is, you can change it. You can make it better. You have to squash that voice in your head that tells you to give up, or worse, just distracts you from your potential.

How many times have you stopped yourself from doing something special because you let your doubts and fears beat your belief? Throughout my career leading teams, I've seen countless people limit themselves. They convince themselves that they can't do something before even making an attempt. They restrict their results by selling themselves short and selling everyone, including themselves, excuses.

Because they don't really believe that they can achieve their potential, their fears and doubts control their actions. Fears and doubts manifest in excuses and distractions.

There is no job security any longer, so just like your business idea can go bust, you can also work for a company for years and be let go a few years before retirement. Then what? Would you have regrets then? As for earning a living or attaining your dreams, not all dreams are about lots of money or money at all for that matter.

Your potential and greatness aren't only measured by your bank account. That is a really narrow way to think about greatness. Your greatness is about going after your best. If you happen to make a lot of money doing it, all the better. The money isn't the why, and your belief isn't about whether you can earn more money. Going after your why and believing you can get it is a huge part of reaching your greatness, simply because it isn't easy and it is what most people avoid. Go after your greatness, in whatever area of life it may be.

Believe. Believe in yourself, your capabilities, your ideas, and your dreams and projects. Believe that you can achieve great success and that you have what it takes. Believe that there is no difference between you and any of the so-called greats. J. K. Rowling, author of the *Harry Potter* series, was poor and had failed over and over before becoming successful. Michael Jordan was cut from his high school basketball team. Abraham Lincoln was a failed businessman and politician before becoming one of the greatest presidents in American history. The world would have never been graced by their talents had they not believed more in their potential than in their failures. They were all just average people who had suffered defeats. What made them special and led to their eventual greatness was actually nothing special at all. They simply didn't stop believing in themselves.

Belief is a simple little quality that can lead to greatness. You have it. Believe you were meant to be great, that you were meant to be a champion. Everyone has greatness in him or her, but most people lack the belief to go and get it.

CHAPTER 6

Third Heartbeat—
Champions Grind

Success only comes before work in the dictionary. In real life, to become a champion, one has to put in consistent hard work.

"Work before glory" is a difficult quality to understand because hard work to one person can be seen as a walk in the park for another. What is hard work? How much effort must be put in for work to qualify as hard? How will you know if what you're doing is enough? Before attempting to answer those questions, let's begin by considering some examples of the work put in by some of the greatest champions of all time.

Three-time NBA champion and perhaps the best shot in NBA history, Larry Bird, exemplified hard work. Every day, in addition to his conditioning drills and team practice, Larry would throw no less than five hundred free throw shots to keep his skills sharp.

Georges St-Pierre, my hometown hero and arguably the best pound-for-pound mixed martial arts fighter in history, would go through grueling training in preparation for a fight. Like all professional fighters, he would prepare aggressively for months before a fight. He would work out twice a day, six days a week for months, in addition to following a strict diet and studying his opponent through video analysis.

What made George St-Pierre special was that he would seek out the best trainers in the world for various disciplines. These disciplines would depend on his competitor. If his opponent were a good boxer, he would train with a boxing coach, in addition to still preparing his other martial arts disciplines, in order to improve. St-Pierre aimed not just to be better than he was, but to be better than his opponent! He consistently took these extra steps that others warranted as unnecessary; however, his track record would say otherwise. Not only was he a long-standing welterweight champion in the Ultimate Fighting Championship, he was known for beating his challengers at their own strength!

Both Larry Bird and George St-Pierre were greats from different eras and sports. Their work ethic and passion to succeed isn't restricted to sports either. All of the most famous successful people in the world have also had similar experiences in order to get to their levels of greatness. They began with a belief in themselves to win and then worked harder than their peers did in order to reach their goals. They didn't stop or give up. To achieve their goals, stopping wasn't an option.

The first important thing to understand about the work needed to become a champion is that stopping isn't an option. You must continue to work every day if you are to attain your full potential. It is in the little things done daily, and not one great thing will get you there.

What if Michael Jordan stopped trying after getting cut from his high school team? Instead he went home, and after wiping away his tears, he got back to work to ensure he would never get cut again. What if Abraham Lincoln accepted his political defeats and business failures and stopped trying to reach his potential? Instead he continued to work and learn until he reached his potential and became sixteenth president of the United States. What if Elon Musk, creator of online financial services company X.com (which eventually became PayPal), Space X, and Tesla Motors, gave up after any of his numerous early business failures?

Champions grind, and *grind* is the perfect term to use when looking at the work ethic of champions. One of the best definitions of the word is as follows, "to move noisily and laboriously, especially against a countering force." When working to achieve your greatness, there are many countering forces: your doubts and fears, the doubts and fears of those you love, and the countering force of life itself. If it were easy, everyone would do it. Champions do it against and in spite of the difficulties. They work consistently, knowing it will all pay off eventually, and until it does, they'll need to continue.

Grinding is all about effort, giving everything you have, and leaving it all out there and knowing that, whether you succeed or fail, there was nothing more that you could have done. Grinding allows champions to always keep their heads high. There is no shame in losing or failing when you've given your best and all of it. There is shame and regret, however, in knowing that you may have lost because you didn't try hard enough.

The thing with effort is that no one can truly judge your effort but you. It is something you take home with you, and in your heart and head, you know when you could have given more. Have you ever tried to do something but pulled back a little because you were afraid of failing? Your fear of failure in essence sabotaged your chances of success. You created your self-fulfilling prophecy, and your Bad Wolf is thankful for it.

But deep down, you knew you could have given that much more, and if you had, you might have succeeded. Talk about feeding your doubts and regrets! Instead you could have given it your all, and even if you would have failed, you would have still been satisfied knowing that you didn't fail because of your efforts.

It is in the effort devoted to your greatness where you will find your satisfaction. If you don't try your hardest, if you don't fight against the countering forces, how can you be satisfied with yourself? You may try to sell yourself some excuses, but you'll know the truth: you lost because of you. But if you try your hardest, really grinding it out in order to succeed, you will be satisfied with your effort, no matter the results.

It is in the grind where most people truly begin loving the person he or she becomes on the path to greatness. It is in facing our fears and overcoming obstacles that we learn to truly learn to respect ourselves. In many ways, it is growing to love the people we become on our journey to greatness where we achieve our greatness.

Distractions

Working hard consistently is extremely difficult, particularly in the increasingly instantaneous world we live in. This makes devoting oneself to a long-term gain increasingly difficult. Think about it: don't like the song you're listening to? Skip it. Don't like the movie you're watching? Go back and select from any of the thousands of others online. Like the show you're watching? No worries, you can stream the whole series tonight instead of waiting for another episode every week.

We live in a world that has forgotten long term and sacrifice. This may be a little funny, but having to listen to a song that you're tired of because the batteries of your Walkman will die if you fast-forward was a first-world problem, but one that still taught us about dealing with (small) consequences to get what we want. Don't get me started with having to rewind a VHS tape before returning it to the video rental place in order to avoid the rewind charge.

Achieving your greatness isn't something that is anything close to instantaneous. It requires a lot of work sustained over an extended period. Anyone can work over a short period. Working as hard as possible until you achieve your dream is something that most people wouldn't be ready to do. That is why uncommon results come from uncommon efforts. If you do what everyone else does, how can you expect to achieve more? Go further? Be better? Become a champion?

Giving your best effort is something that takes time to learn. For example, when an athlete begins a new workout regimen, he or she works hard. However, at times the athlete will feel afterward that he or she still had a little more in the tank to give. Perhaps from complacency or learning to pace himself or herself correctly, the athlete took his or her foot off the gas.

The greats reflect on why they hadn't shown up and adjusted. That reflection and learning leads them to give more and more consistently and eventually leads them to be the best at their discipline. Michael Jordan, Wayne Gretzky, Kobe Bryant, Conor McGregor, Tiger Woods, Roger Federer, Lionel Messi, Cristiano Ronaldo, and Rafael Nadal all trained harder than any of their competitors did when at the top of their game.

They say that the mind gives up long before your muscles do when you're training physically. It is the same when doing any kind of difficult work. As you work toward your goals, you will hit bumps in the road, some bigger than others. Setbacks and failures will knock you back and knock you down. Life will get in the way and try to convince you that you're better off giving up—that it was a bad idea in the first place and that you don't have what it takes.

That voice in you is your doubts and fears, trying to make you stop believing and trying. When the going gets tough and the easy path calls to you, when people around you begin to question you and your capabilities to succeed, it is in those moments that you will want to quit most. Stopping will find the support of doubters, haters, and your Bad Wolf. It is in those moments that champions work even harder. They continue not only despite the doubts and fears but because of them. It is what separates the greats from the rest. It is what allows them to succeed because they continue when the average person would stop.

So the championship quality of work is simple: work harder than the next guy or gal and don't stop until you reach your goal ... until you're a champion.

CHAPTER 7

Fourth Heartbeat—
Champions Never Settle

Champions work hard on their path to greatness, not stopping despite setbacks, failures, criticism, doubts, and fears. By working hard, specifically harder than their peers, people will automatically improve, hence the 10,000-hour rule. It is the reference to the number of hours someone needs to dedicate to practicing a certain skill before it is mastered. It is attributed in large part to the success of people like Bill Gates and Steve Jobs, who both obsessively worked on computers and programming, starting in their high school years. Both eventually became giants in the world. Golf great Tiger Woods played more golf than any other amateur for years, starting at age four! By the time he was a teen, he had played way more than 10,000 hours and began his domination of the sport for years.

So putting in the hours is undoubtedly important. Except champions don't just want to get better. They want to be the best. There are days where they know they didn't get their best results or didn't put in their finest efforts. Just like there will be days where we get the outputs we were hoping for and others when we don't. What makes you a great or not is what do you do about it when you have one of those bad days? When you don't meet your expectations, do you turn a blind eye to it? Champions don't; greats don't.

But let's frame it a different way. What would you do if someone you were paying from your pocket wasn't meeting your expectations? Imagine it is your landscaper, cleaning lady, or even your dry cleaner. What would you do? Imagine your dry cleaner did a poor job pressing your shirts. Imagine your house looked the same way after your cleaning service left as it did before they got there. I'm sure you would not be happy and would expect an improvement in the quality of service, or you'd take your business elsewhere!

What do you do when you let yourself down? Do you expect an improvement of services? Do you take your business elsewhere? Of course not. Too often people allow it to go on like they don't have a choice. However, if you've decided to go after your greatness, to reach for your full potential, you already know that you do have a choice that life doesn't have to be the way it is and it won't if you don't want it. It's the choice to take charge of your life and go after your fire!

Champions are their own hardest critics. They are much harder on themselves than they are on anyone else or by anyone else. With the desire to be the best, greats can't afford to go easy on themselves because they know their competition won't. In life, regardless of what you're aiming to reach your potential in, the path won't take it easy on you either. To become great, to be successful, and to be better than your peers, it requires honest introspection. With it, champions then adjust their path to get past whatever is holding them back. We can do the same in everyday life.

Imagine you work on the road, meeting with clients, and one day are stuck in so much traffic that you end up arriving late to all three of your appointments, one of which was canceled when you finally got there. Do you just chalk it up to bad luck? Was it out of your control so there was nothing that could have been done? Perhaps … or perhaps you're only partly right. What if you rerouted your appointments so you're travelling against traffic throughout the day, scheduled meetings closer together so it is easier to make it to each one on time, or spread them out further in the day?

The point is, if you chalk it up to bad luck, you've done nothing but let yourself off the hook. How many times would you let your dry cleaner get away with messing up the pressing of your shirts before you said something? How many times before you went elsewhere? It is the same idea. If you have expectations for your day, workout, meeting, or month, you should evaluate as you go, as well as after it is done. Often it is a simple mental review of how things went, why you feel that way (making sure you're being as objective as possible), and what you can do to either correct the issue the next time or repeat the effort and performance. The more you can do that, the better you will get faster.

History books are full of stories of people, companies, and empires who overestimated their advantages and underestimated their competition. Upset stories are always fan favorites because everyone loves to cheer on the underdog. Underdog stories highlight the flaws in the favorite's thinking and how the underdog capitalized on weaknesses. Buster Douglas was supposed to be a speed bump for Mike Tyson, but he had a reason that pushed him harder than the champ did. Mike Tyson's corner didn't even bring ice because they didn't expect to need it. They were sure it would be an easy fight for Iron Mike.

The 1980 American Olympic men's ice hockey team was dubbed the "Miracle on Ice" for beating the heavy favorite Russian team. The Russian team had won six of the last seven Olympic gold medals in men's ice hockey and were packed with professional players, versus a team of college kids from the United States. Coach Herb Brooks led the American men to a 4-3 upset win of the USSR and eventually to the gold medal win against Finland.

These are two famous examples, but sports are full of them, and that's why so many people love sports. Underdogs in life are often less dramatic about it, but there are tons of their stories too. One of my favorites since learning it is that of Theodore Roosevelt, the twenty-sixth president of the United States. Born in 1858, Teddy was seen as a weak child due to asthma and nearsightedness. In those days, boys were expected to help out physically around the home, which led to Theodore's father's disappointment.

In response, young Roosevelt committed to living a "strenuous life," where each day is lived with vigor and conviction. He put fearlessness as a constant goal on his list. He took up doing weights, hiking, and boxing. In college, he boxed competitively and took up rowing, and then he climbed a mountain to the displeasure of his doctor, who worried that his heart could not support the "strenuous lifestyle" Roosevelt was living.

This approach to life, of not accepting current conditions and challenging them, took Theodore Roosevelt to the presidency of the United States, an unthinkable destiny considering his early prognosis. Champions don't accept status quos. They know that what got them this far will not be enough to keep them going. What won yesterday may win today but won't again tomorrow. Competition gets better, challenges get harder, and obstacles get bigger. For every level, there is another devil, and to keep moving forward, champions do more than they did before. Remember the old saying, "If you always do what you've always done, you'll always get what you've always got." Napoleon Hill said once, "Strength and growth come only through continuous effort and struggle."

Warren Buffet said this about business,

> The one thing that is absolutely sure to kill a business is complacency. Being comfortable with where you are, thinking your current effort is sufficient. That it's enough ... it isn't and if you get comfortable, someone willing to pay a steeper price will come along and take what's yours. And there is always someone working hard to do just that.

It is a great quote that doesn't only apply to business, but to any team and person looking to succeed. In business, it is said that it's like a moving sidewalk that is going the wrong way. If you're not working to move forward, you're slipping backward. This also applies to people on the road to success. Not only do you need to believe and work hard, you must work hard at continuously improving if you're to make it to your objective. This is simple to see when you are competing against another person or team. You must continuously be better than you were the day before if you want to beat your adversary.

Another example is when you are competing against an unseen opponent, for instance, a manufacturer from another country or when you are working to move up the corporate ladder. Your colleagues are, to a certain extent, your unseen adversary. It can also be the voices in your head telling you to pull back on the reins, an unseen opponent. Regardless of the opponent, complacency is sure to dash any hope of succeeding.

To be able to constantly improve is slightly easier when evaluating straightforward objectives or targets. For example, I once had a bet with my boss at the time as to who could increase his maximum number of push-ups. We had one month to prepare. Every day I trained, and I could evaluate if I were doing more than the number I had begun at. I could easily tell on a week-to-week basis if I were getting better.

Unfortunately life isn't always so linear and single-tracked. You will have bad days where your performance suffers. You will have other priorities that knock you off track. These things happen all the time. Champions brush them off and keep going. Again, you simply need to accept the setbacks, learn from them, and keep moving forward.

When things are going well, people will often become complacent, allowing their ego to convince them that they're doing enough. That's why Brian Tracy said, "Good is the enemy of great." It is why so many people, teams, and companies fail! They begin to allow ego to take over. They believe that what they're doing is enough and can continue to be enough.

Or worse, as I've seen with leading salespeople, they begin cutting out the things that made them successful in the first place. They start believing in mystical things like talent and destiny and forget about hard facts like hard work and continuous improvement. There is no shortcutting the game on the road to greatness. As Michael Jordan once said, "If you shortcut the game, the game is going to shortcut you."

The second threat is ineffective self-monitoring. To consistently improve, you have to know yourself. You have to know your strengths and weaknesses so you can take actions to build upon your strengths and improve your shortcomings. As George St-Pierre would work to improve himself on his opponents' strengths, the champion has to constantly self-monitor to find the chink in their armor. If you've ever worked for (even) a somewhat organized manager, you have experienced the performance appraisal. As a human resource director, I've designed and done many appraisals. The evaluations are designed to achieve two objectives, one of them being to provide summary feedback to the employee on his or her performance. Champions perform their own performance appraisals on a regular basis.

Without honest self-analysis and feedback, it is very difficult (if not impossible) to know what to improve on and how. You could be working hard to shore up your defenses while leaving a gaping hole on your flank that your enemy can walk through unmolested.

Constant improvement is hard, but no one said success and greatness would be easy. The process is beset with frustration and setbacks as consistent improvement isn't, as mentioned earlier, a linear process. It happens in ebbs and waves and isn't something that can be evaluated on a daily basis. Improvement is a lengthy process, which is why so few people make it to greatness. Your why and your belief have to be strong enough to be able to continue working hard over the long term, despite setbacks.

Kaizen—The Rule of 1 Percent

The Japanese call the process of continuous improvement *Kaizen*. It is the process that they followed after World War II that eventually made their products, from cars to electronics, the best in the world. It is the process that is now emulated in many of the best companies in the world. It isn't only a process reserved for companies either. All teams and people can apply its principles. As opposed to working on attaining your big, nasty, gnarly goal, eating the proverbial elephant at once, you simply need to break it down into tiny goals. Or eat the elephant one bite at a time. With Kaizen, the goal is to improve by 1 percent every day.

When we focus on the end goal, we can easily become overwhelmed and discouraged. An early setback or two can leave you with the hopeless feeling of having such a long way to go, as if you'll never make it. Break that big, nasty, gnarly goal down into small, edible chunks, and now it doesn't seem so impossible. It no longer appears like a massive mountain. The process of Kaizen dictates that you break it into chunks of chunks so you can feel the progress so you can celebrate the victories, albeit small ones, with positivity and motivation to succeed again the next day.

The psychology behind it is simple: succeeding is addictive. The more wins you stack up, the more you want to stack. I had always heard about breaking down goals in order to succeed and avoid quitting because the big, nasty goal was still too far off. The concept of 1 percent hit home when I began training for Spartan Races. I was already in good shape, but I'd need to build my cardio and endurance further if I'd have a chance at completing the thirteen-plus-kilometer obstacle course. I needed to add jogging to my workout routine.

There was only one problem: I really hated jogging. I was more of a natural sprinter, short and stalky. Endurance running wasn't my thing. But I needed to do it, so I began jogging. I wanted to start by running for thirty minutes, but I had trouble getting past the ten-minute mark because I'd start thinking about how much time was left, particularly as I'd start to feel some fatigue in my legs. I had trouble, and it wasn't with my muscles either. It was in my head.

I had trouble until I spoke with a friend who loves jogging. He told me to focus only on the next step. He instructed me to forget about the time of the full distance. That's why apps and GPS watches were made. Just focus on the next step. Right, left, right, left. I only had to make one more step, then another, and another. With that simple piece of advice, everything changed. I went from three-kilometer runs to five-kilometer runs. I managed to get my five-kilometer time to under thirty minutes. Then I finished ten kilometers in fifty minutes. Now I can run a half marathon, and I love running because I enter my world where all I need to think about is the next step.

Kaizen is the same. Focus on improving by 1 percent over yesterday. You won't be able to do it every day, but when you don't, you only have to return to get better by 1 percent. You don't have to look up and see a massive mountain of a goal ahead.

One percent may seem too easy, too small, to amount to anything. First, you're hopefully in the success business for the long haul. Regardless, 1 percent may start out small, which is great as you build your confidence and get used to improving in what you're doing. As you improve, the 1 percent compounds (1 percent of ten is one-tenths while 1 percent of one thousand is ten), and you will make bigger strides toward achieving success. Think of it as building momentum, just as an airplane builds speed as it tears down the runway toward takeoff.

What's great about Kaizen is that it reinforces the idea that the path to success doesn't end. Without wanting to sound too corny, there is a lot of truth in the maxim, "Success isn't a destination; it's a journey." Success is the journey. You're already a champion when you commit to improving every day, and you will feel it. There is a great quote I once read by Rory Vaden, "Success isn't owned. It's rented. And the rent is due every day."

The Sigmoid Curve

Constant improvement is necessary, but as we continue to improve, there will also come the need for change.

Eventually your improvements in certain areas will dwindle, and how you approach those areas will need to change in order to continue to progress. It can be in relation to anything in your improvement. So while change can be improvement, modification also represents a different approach or direction.

Allow me to again use physical fitness as an example. As I work out and get better regularly, at some point, if I continue to use the same training methods, I will plateau. To avoid the plateau, I will need to change my workouts. You'll see this with professional athletes who, despite doing well, will change their coach or trainer. They do so because they feel that they just aren't improving any more. The same would apply to anything that you are seeking to improve constantly. Eventually you will peak, and you will need to change in order to continue progress.

The principle of the sigmoid curve is one that applies to things that enjoy a life cycle, including products, relationships, teams, companies, empires, personal progress, and even life itself. Your progress on the road to success will also have a life cycle as you will need to adapt and change the realities around you. The s-shaped curve depicts how things begin, then rise, and, at a given point, decline. If that decline is not corrected, the end is not far behind.

Take, for example, a local eatery. Generally restaurants open and scrape by as they build their reputations and get more customers. The early days are particularly difficult as budgets are limited and money is tight. This early stage, the learning stage, translates to bad service if the restaurant gets unexpectedly busy.

But as time goes on, the well-run business manager adapts, adjusts, and manages to impress customers enough to return. As they build their names and customer bases, sales and (normally) profits increase. This stage is known as the growth stage. The increases continue until people begin to tire of their recipe, until the business reaches its peak. Maybe the décor becomes dated, or perhaps competition simply outdoes the menu.

As people tire, the restaurant must reinvent itself to reenergize its clients. If they wait too long, as the business enters the decline stage, it will take a lot more effort to recapture all of the clients who've already decided to go elsewhere. Change may come too soon, during the learning stage or early in the growth stage. People who enjoyed the original recipe may be disappointed, and the restaurant may not maximize its cycle.

The sigmoid curve is different for every situation. Each curve will have differences in the stages. Keeping with businesses, some will have very short learning curves followed by extremely long growth stages, then followed by a very quick and sharp decline. Others will experience short growth stages and very slow declines. Then there are those that do not enter decline because changes are made before the cycle peaks and the momentum from the growth stage is carried into the learning stage of the next cycle.

The sigmoid curve shows us that timing is everything. A properly timed change will allow for maximization of the cycle and will avoid unneeded effort to right the course. Whether it be for a team or an individual, improvements and change must come while there is still momentum, during the growth stage. Without the momentum, it will require a lot more effort to start a cycle over again.

I am not saying that change shouldn't take place at a later stage. Of course it should, but you should always be evaluating your progress in order to avoid needing to exert more effort than necessary to improve. The road to success and the need for constant improvement is difficult enough as it is. Evaluating your progress is needed to avoid making the road even more difficult whenever change is needed.

So what about when you attain your big, nasty, gnarly goal? Don't stop! Maintain what you've done to get there and self-monitor to see where you can go for another 1 percent and another 1 percent and another. Find other areas where you, your team, or your business can reach new heights. Go for it! There is no arriving. The champion isn't ready to lose simply because he or she is at the top. Champions want to keep winning. They want to remain champion. In life like in business, we do not have a pinnacle. Being a champion is how we approach the journey. A champion approaches it every day, trying to improve on the previous day and never settling.

CHAPTER 8

Fifth Heartbeat—
Champions Are Obsessed
with Being Champion

"Greatness in anything requires obsession."

—*CT Fletcher*

Will Smith, Conor McGregor, Steve Jobs, Bill Gates, Michael Jordan, Michael Phelps, George Soros, Sydney Crosby, Eric Thomas, CT Fletcher, and more all became great successes because they were obsessed with succeeding. Becoming the best didn't happen by accident. It required for them to work harder and sacrifice more than their competition and their peers. They reached their full potential by making success the only available option. To perform at that level, to be the best you can possibly be at whatever fuels your fire, you need to make it a top priority in life. Talent and desires aren't enough. Skills and goals aren't enough either. It wasn't enough for any of the greats mentioned, and it won't be enough for you. If you are to reach your full potential, you will need to become obsessed with doing so.

Before I continue, many people could argue that obsession is bad, that it is unhealthy. I've had people call me crazy because of how hard I work and push myself to improve and succeed. Personally, I don't think any less would be good enough in order to be my best. That said, I also agree that there can be an unhealthy level of obsession. For example, there's the girl who wants to be a model and develops eating disorders so she can try to feel thin enough. Or there's the workaholic who neglects his family by pouring all of the energy and attention into his work.

These are unhealthy examples of obsession because they eventually lead to negative repercussions. Wanting to be a champion in life and reaching your potential aren't short-term goals. They are goals that we spend our lives seeking because they reward us while pursuing them. It also isn't enough to become the best. Success means continuing to be the best that you can be.

Furthermore, being a champion in life isn't one-dimensional. Who wants to be rich and loathed? Healthy and poor? Loved by some and hated by the rest? We all want it all! We want to succeed in our work. We have enough money to support our lifestyles, loving friends and family, and good health. That is what champions need to aspire to.

Conor McGregor is the current UFC lightweight champion. Most know him for his swag and big mouth. His style and demeanor are typical of the type of fighter I want knocked into the third row, except he is different. Despite his bravado, he does an awesome job at backing it up—not only with his fighting but also with his reasoning. I started to like Conor when listening to him talk about his mental preparation and how his belief and hard work would lead him to be champion.

Most impressive perhaps was when his career was just starting out. At his early record of four and one, he spoke of his belief that his hard work and obsession would lead him to become the UFC champion. It's always impressive to an outsider when someone predicts his or her own success, but neither impressive nor surprising to the person succeeding.

In a more recent interview, Conor spoke of his obsession with greatness and how everything related to his dream in his head 24/7. The interviewer asked him whether his obsession was unhealthy, to which McGregor responded, "To me what's unhealthy is living an unhealthy life. To me what's unhealthy is getting up and going to the same job everyday of your life, 9-5 in an office. That's unhealthy! That beats your mind! I don't work, I love what I do."

This healthy obsession required of champions is one that provides joy and pleasure. It relates to their passion so it completely engulfs them. It is well known that, when someone engages in something that he or she enjoys, finds challenging, and is passionate about, this person can become completely engulfed in his or her work where he or she performs at a much higher level of intensity. People have called it being in the zone or in flow. And when people can get in the zone, they become much more likely to learn more, do more, and succeed.

Bill Gates would program overnight and more than twenty hours every weekend while in high school. By the time he was in college, he had accumulated more experience than most professional programmers of the time. Will Smith said, "I've never really considered myself as particularly talented. Where I excel is ridiculous, sickening work ethic."

Phil Jackson, Michael Jordan's coach for eight seasons, said, "He takes nothing about the game for granted." And "there's a certain humility in Michael's willingness to take on the difficult work of making himself a more complete player. For me, one of the signs of Michael's greatness is that he turned his weaknesses into strengths." Throughout his career, Michael Jordan was always considered one of the hardest-working players in the NBA. Some would say despite being the best; others would say as a result of it.

To become great, to reach your full potential, you must be laser-guided on where you're going and what you must do to get there. All greats don't waste time on things that don't help them achieve their goals and their greatness. What about things that aren't on their crucial path? They either eliminate them altogether, and if they can't, they find a way to get them done quickly or for someone else to do it for them.

If you want to be great, if you want to achieve your full potential, you're going to have to do what others don't and won't. This may mean waking up at 5:00 a.m. to get a leg up on the competition. Or it may mean forgoing parties in college to get more practice or have more time to work on your goals. It isn't a coincidence that companies like FedEx and Facebook were created by people who ended up quitting school after starting up their amazing projects while studying. Remember, common efforts don't turn into uncommon results.

The essence of champions being obsessed with being champion can be found in a quote by CT Fletcher, ex-world weightlifting champion, "You may have been born with more genetic prowess than I have, but you cannot out determine me! You can't out-will me, you can't out want me. You can't out work me, you can't out-desire me!" It is said that you cannot beat someone who doesn't give up. If your only focus, your only possible outcome, is succeeding, how can you be stopped?

This doesn't mean that working on your goal is the only thing you do. Few of us are lucky enough to be UFC champions who work in our passion, meaning you will have to dedicate time and energy to other things too like work, family, and friends, regular stuff.

You may not be able to only work on your goal, and that may not be a bad thing. Being obsessed and only doing that one thing can easily become unhealthy. But being obsessed means that everything you see and do is tinted and influenced by your obsession, your dream.

I can honestly say that this champion's heartbeat has been the hardest quality to write about because it is all heart. It is illogical. The fact is that anyone who isn't on the path will think your obsession is crazy. They'll tell you that it's unhealthy. Your friends will think you're ditching them when you work on your thing instead of theirs. You'll stop doing the things that aren't important to you, to your greatness. Because it's so hard to explain, let me provide you with some examples.

Part of my path to greatness includes physical training. I think everyone should make it part of his or her daily routines for the strength benefits it provides the body and mind. My training routine is rigorous, the harder the better. The more I sweat and the more my muscles scream for me to stop, the happier I am with my efforts. It's obsession. When I go out and see that drinks are being served, I think about my training routine for the following day and usually decline because I'd rather not have that one drink and negatively impact my performance the next day. That's obsession. When I eat, I think about the fuel I am putting in my body and how it impacts my output. That's obsession. I'd rather get my sleep and feel as if I could run a marathon than stay up for a night to be forgotten. That's obsession.

It's easiest to exemplify with physical training, but the same applies for my life goals. I write every day for at least fifteen minutes. That's obsession. I am always on the lookout for material, stories, or articles that could add to this book. That's obsession. I constantly look at how I'm working and evaluate and plan to ensure I'm doing things as best possible. I evaluate to make sure I'm improving and advancing. I revise my progress to ensure that my ladder to success is still leaning on the correct wall. That's obsession. I'm always learning by reading books, magazines, and articles; watching videos; talking to people; and listening to people. That's obsession. That's constant improvement, 1 percent at a time. That's not settling or being content. In fact, it's being disappointed when I'm not improving or when I feel like I didn't work as hard or do as well as I could or should have.

If you want to be the best, if you want to reach the summit, you must be obsessed with becoming the best. It won't happen by mistake. You won't hit the target without aiming. There aren't two ways about it. Greatness in any domain, in any sphere, can't be achieved without obsession. People will tell you that obsession is a bad thing, but how is just getting by your whole life supposed to be good for you? It's not.

I feel as if I've rambled a little, but that demonstrates obsession—illogical, passionate heart. It is that emotional devotion to a purpose that is greater than you are. It is a dedication to be something that you couldn't be without it. It is the burning flame that lights your way to your dreams. It is the flame that without, when the journey would get tough, would be too dark to continue. Obsession is the fire inside that burns hot and fuels your engine. It is the voice in your soul that responds to the Bad Wolf when he says that you're not strong enough to weather the storm. "I am the storm." Be obsessed.

The Reticular Activating System (RAS)

They say that we are whatever we think of most. It is said that, if you think positive and really feel it, you'll attract it. If you think negative, you will attract negative. While that remains debatable, there is no debating that we will be attracted to whatever we think of the most. The reticular activating system (RAS) is responsible for recognizing patterns, making sense of things going on, and proving your beliefs by finding supporting evidence. It's the part that explains why a pregnant woman suddenly notices other pregnant woman where she never did before.

Have you ever wanted to buy a new car? Did you notice that, as you set your heart on that car, you began to notice it everywhere? You didn't notice so many before. Why are you seeing so many all of a sudden? You begin to notice what you're thinking of because your RAS is looking for evidence to show you in order to support your belief.

Being obsessed with your success works in many ways the same way as wanting to buy that new BMW you've been saving for. So imagine that, instead of seeing five-thirty-fives at every corner, you begin seeing people who are doing what you want to do and are succeeding. You also see opportunities for growth or advancement toward your goals.

When you want something really badly and you work at it daily, it will occupy your thoughts. There are two ways that it can occupy your thoughts:

1. The positive way: you think of it as a motivation, and it brings happiness.
2. The negative way: you ruminate and stress, even until health is negatively impacted.

When you're going after something that you believe in with a solid why, it is so much easier to remain positive. If you have these motivated, positive thoughts constantly on the top of your mind, you'll tend to be happier. You will be more likely to see change and anything new as opportunities, which would allow you to a higher likelihood of capitalizing on them versus seeing change as threatening.

Recognizing the opportunities as such combined with the right fuel for your motivation and the belief that you can do it will lead to a higher possibility in trying and therefore in succeeding. As you succeed more, you will be more driven, and you will think more about your target. It is a self-fueling cycle that basically goes, the more you think of succeeding, the more you recognize opportunities, the more you try, the more you succeed, and repeat.

Obsessed on Success and Being Laser-Guided

Be laser-guided on your potential, dreams, and goals. Eliminate the excuses that low performers provide to make their lack of results acceptable, normally to remove all responsibility for their poor performance. Ignore the excuses or move past them. Make growth and improvement nonnegotiable musts in your life. Seek knowledge and growth that will propel you forward toward your goals. Make the commitment not to settle. Become obsessed with improving on your past results, no matter how good they are.

Make your obsession with growth, improvement, and your greatness a large part of your daily routine. Aim high and work harder than everyone else to hit the target. Have it on your radar every day; make it something you are constantly evaluating and working on. Celebrate each win, and then move on and look to each setback or loss as an opportunity for future growth.

CHAPTER 9

Becoming a Champion

The road to greatness is not a smooth one. It is bumpy, filled with obstacles, consistently an uphill battle, and lined with naysayers and doubters. It is dark and lonely. It isn't an easy road to travel along, but if it were easy, everyone would do it. If you picked up this book, you are likely already on your way. You at the very least have begun to awaken to your potential and are now looking for motivation and guidance on how to reach it. Or at best, you are already a very successful person who is simply getting a recharge of the motivation battery. Either way, whether you're at the start of your journey or long into it, it is a constant challenge. Regardless of how motivated you are today, you will need to recharge again soon to keep going.

Have Fuel for Your Fire: Know Your Why

With the right fuel, your why (your motivation) will last longer than someone with a superficial reason to go for his or her goal. Properly processing your motivations with a technique like the five whys is a great way to clarify to yourself the real motivation of embarking on the difficult path. The stronger the fuel, the brighter the flame, and the easier it is to starve the Bad Wolf.

Most importantly, you'll need a very strong internal reason to go for it since you may not get the support you'd like from your friends and loved ones. While they may support you at first, our loved ones will often discourage us out of concern for us once they see how difficult it is. Others won't understand your why as you do, so they won't understand the need to keep going when the going gets tough. Find your why, and make it absolutely clear to yourself why success is the only option. Remind yourself constantly why you've chosen not to take the easy path. Keep your fire burning bright and hot, and you'll make it!

Believe in Yourself: Believe in Your Greatness

Remember that everything around us was created by people who were no smarter or greater than you are. Success and greatness are not reserved for a select few. The kings and queens of history were not chosen by anyone but themselves. They are and were no different than any of us. The best investors, top CEOs, best rap stars, and renowned actors are not special. They are not a special breed. They are cut from the same cloth of all of us. They have simply dedicated their time and effort toward their dreams and potential. You can do the same, and if you do, you too can reach your potential. You have what it takes. We all do.

Remember that, while everyone has what it takes to reach his or her full potential, most people lack the belief in themselves to do it. You will be different. You're taking steps to succeed that others don't. You know that, with the right fuel, work ethic, and determination, there is absolutely no reason why you won't succeed. Keep in mind that all of the greats experienced failure earlier on in their careers and in their lives, and if they had stopped believing in themselves, you would never have heard about them. Believe in yourself, even in your failures. Failing simply means that you need to find another way to do it, but you can figure it out! Remind yourself regularly, "Yes, I can!"

Work Hard ... Every Day

There is no substitute for elbow grease, and the fact is that your dreams, goals, and plans won't work if you don't. Their success will be a direct result of your effort. Dreams remain figments of our imagination without the work needed to make them reality. Grind. When the Bad Wolf starts chirping about giving up, about how it is too hard or not worth it, don't stop. Keep grinding. Find people on the same path as you and work as hard or harder than them. Don't let up until you arrive, and then after a brief pause, get back on track.

The thought of hard work scares off a lot of people from going after their dreams. This is truly unfortunate because the hard work makes the journey most rewarding. While I've mentioned a few times that, if it were easy, everyone would do it, I should add that, if it were easy, it also wouldn't be very rewarding. The hard work, which you determine on your path toward success, allows you to grow as a person. That is what makes the journey truly rewarding. Whether you succeed or fail in achieving your goals, the person you become by working hard for your goals is the biggest reward of all.

Never Settle

The path toward your potential shouldn't be a short journey. It is one that can continue until the end of your days. The person you become when you reach your potential is someone who has grown along the way. Much like a diamond is forged through great pressure, you will become a better person through dedication, belief, and hard work. Once you arrive, that person will aspire to be something better.

Matthew McConaughey best explained this upon accepting the People's Choice Award for best actor. He told a story about his path to success through a discussion with one of his mentors when he was a younger man. The mentor asked, whom he aspired to be, to which McConaughey responded, "I aspire to be me in ten years."

Years later, his mentor asked if he had reached his goal, to which McConaughey responded, "Not even close! I'm aiming to be me in ten years." McConaughey then explained how seeking your potential isn't a process that ends. We should always be aspiring to be better than who we were yesterday, who we are today, and who we will be tomorrow. Strive to improve, even if by only 1 percent per day. Nonlinear growth, but progressive growth. Make the commitment to never settle.

Become Obsessed with Success

What do you want? What is your goal? Make that your priority. Make that your crucial path. Everything else is noise that takes your time and energy in the wrong direction. You may not be able to eliminate all of the noise as you may need to work a day job while pursuing your dream. This makes the decision of how you use the rest of your time so important.

Stay focused on remaining on your crucial path. Some people falsely believe that I am prescribing to work nonstop, and this is wrong. If you need to take a break to recharge your batteries, then you're still acting while taking your goals into account. If you're going out one evening with your buddies, this isn't necessarily off your path either. Maintaining healthy relationships is important to your well-being. Besides, you'll need some people to celebrate with you when you make it.

Just keep your dreams a priority in your decisions of how you use your time and energy. Understand how much you need to give to succeed and give it. Don't allow time wasters and low performers to drag you off your path. Being obsessed with success means making your dream the focus and sticking to the plan you've set out to achieve it.

Closing

Congratulations! You are on your way. I hope that your path will be as long, exciting, and rewarding as you deserve. And you only deserve what you put in. I've been on my path for several years and will continue until the very end, and I wish the same for you. My road has been bumpy and curvy, as will yours. At times, it has been very slow going and, at others, very fast paced. All we can do is continue grinding along our path, keep working our plans, and believe that our work will bring us exactly where we need to be.

You are now on your way. You have an idea of what you'll need to do to make it where you want to go. You will truly understand it as you progress further along. It will be easy at times and impossible at others. That is a certainty.

The other certainty is that it is possible. You can do it. I know it, and so should you. Even when you are really feeling down and doubting yourself, when you are incapable to say that you will certainly make it, just tell yourself that it is possible. You already have everything it takes. You are cut from the same cloth as emperors and kings, billionaires, and world-class champions. You can also be great. It is possible. It is all up to you.

Best of luck, champion!

CPSIA information can be obtained
at www.ICGtesting.com
Printed in the USA
LVHW040219190419
614733LV00001B/1/P